The summer sun shone through Jack's window. He
jumped out of bed, threw on his bright red
shirt, and put on his bathing suit. He raced downstairs,
faster than a hound dog after a rabbit.
"Today is my birthday!" Jack announced when he saw his parents.
"And you know what that means!"
His parents smiled.
"We're going to Perkins Cove!"
Every year on Jack's birthday and at Christmas,
Jack went to Perkins Cove to visit his grandmother.
Jack loved to listen to the stories Nana told year after year.
His favorite story was "The Fisherman."

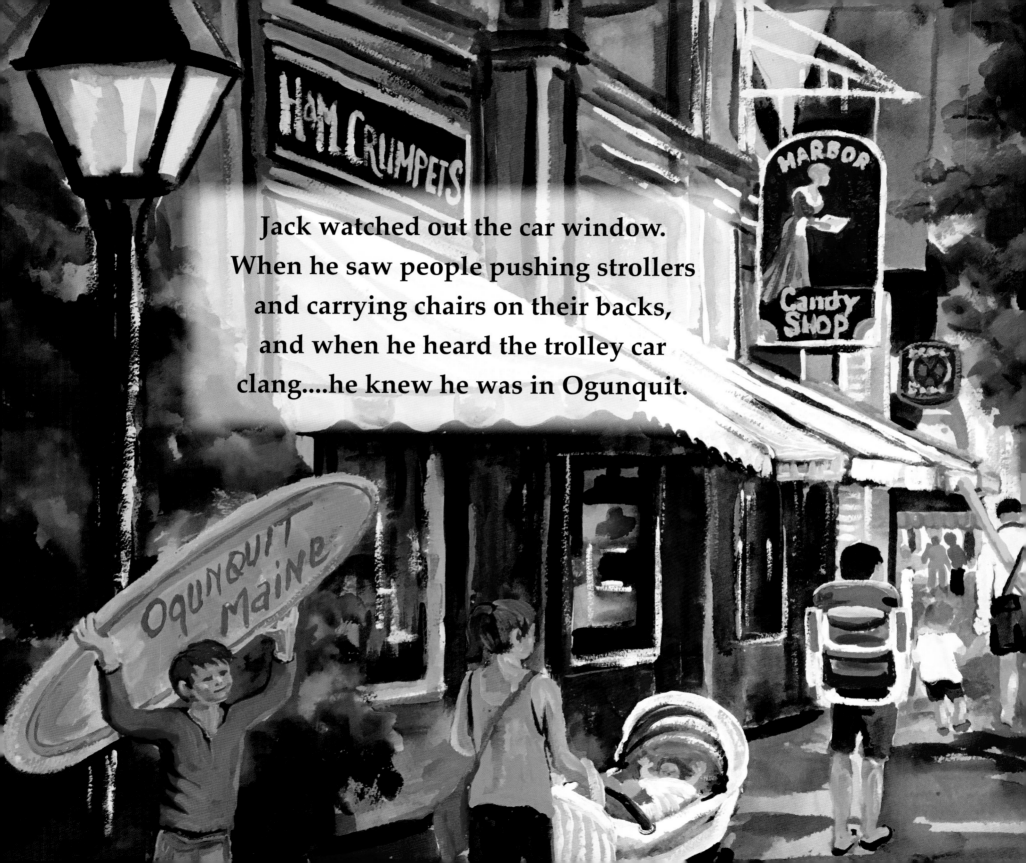

Jack watched out the car window.
When he saw people pushing strollers
and carrying chairs on their backs,
and when he heard the trolley car
clang....he knew he was in Ogunquit.

Jack and his family passed the Perkins Cove sign and turned into Nana's driveway. There she was, waiting with open arms. Jack hugged his nana. "Look how you've grown!" she said, sizing him up. "Tell me the story, Nana. You know; the one about your grandfather, "The Fisherman." Jack sat down beside Nana to listen to her story once again.

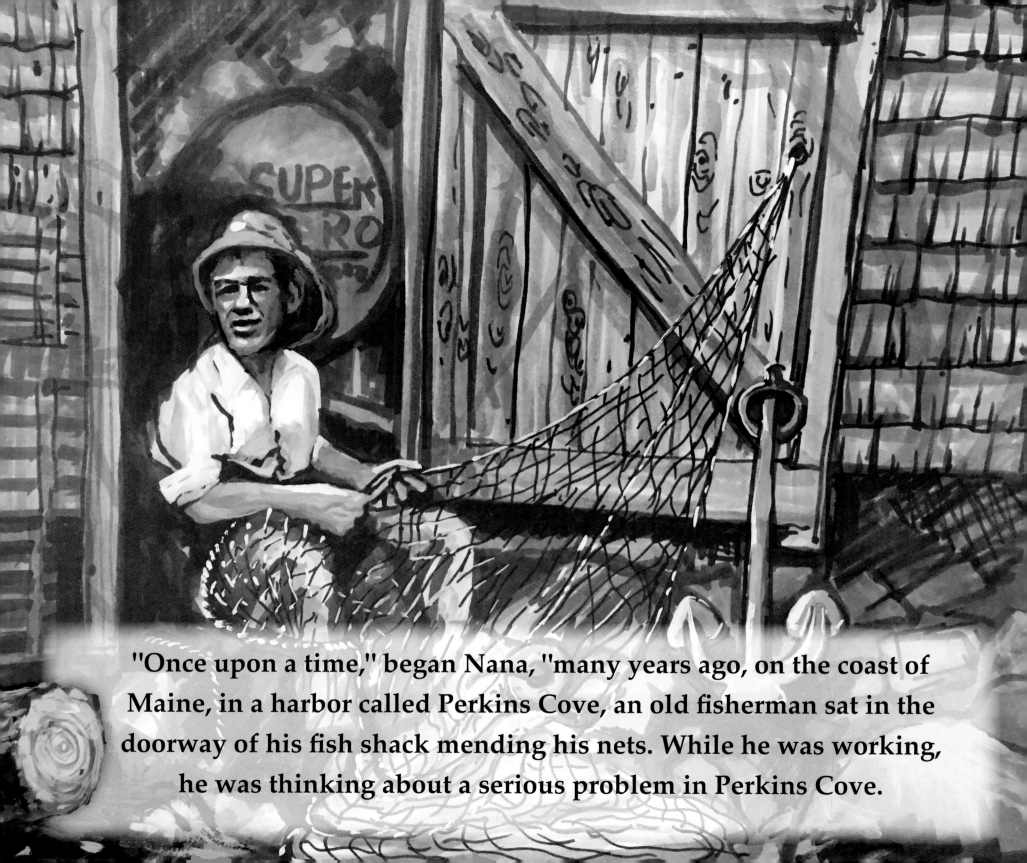

"Once upon a time," began Nana, "many years ago, on the coast of Maine, in a harbor called Perkins Cove, an old fisherman sat in the doorway of his fish shack mending his nets. While he was working, he was thinking about a serious problem in Perkins Cove.

"The Josias River flowed through the village
of Ogunquit and emptied into the cove.

" In the winter fresh water from the river mixed with salty ocean water, causing it to freeze. One day in the spring when the ice began to melt, the tide came in and broke the ice into giant pieces. When the tide went out, big chunks of ice destroyed the footbridge that went across the cove's entrance.

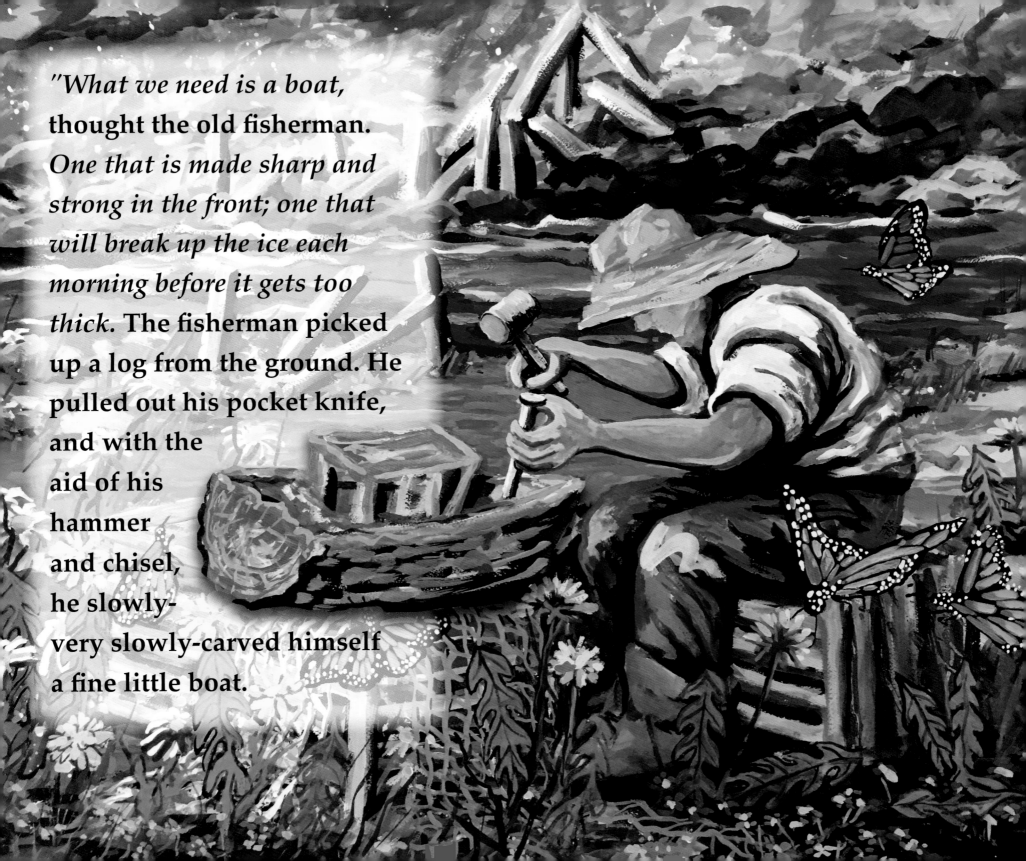

"*What we need is a boat,*
thought the old fisherman.
One that is made sharp and
strong in the front; one that
will break up the ice each
morning before it gets too
thick. The fisherman picked
up a log from the ground. He
pulled out his pocket knife,
and with the
aid of his
hammer
and chisel,
he slowly-
very slowly-carved himself
a fine little boat.

"He painted his boat bright red so it could be easily spotted. The fisherman carved a secret compartment inside, a perfect place to put a hidden treasure, perhaps a seashell or   a pretty piece of seaglass.

"If we had a boat like this, only much bigger, we could break the ice up every morning and never have to worry about the bridge being taken out again, he thought. The fisherman talked to the townspeople, who all agreed it would be a perfect solution. The townspeople set to work to build a boat. With any luck it would be ready by winter.

They called their boat...
"The Crusher"

"The old fisherman was proud of his idea. The town honored him at a special ceremony, giving him a plaque and a shiny brass key to *"The Crusher."* He placed the key in the hidden compartment of the boat he carved and set the boat on the windowsill of his fish shack.

"When my granddaughter comes to visit I'll give it to her, he thought. But one day strong winds from an ocean storm blew the boat right off the windowsill, down the rocky beach, and into rough ocean waters.

"The fisherman carefully searched along the coast for his lost little boat.

"He scoured through the seaside gardens, wishing with all of his heart he could find the boat he had worked so hard to make. But he never did."

Jack also wondered what could
have happened to the boat the
fisherman carved.

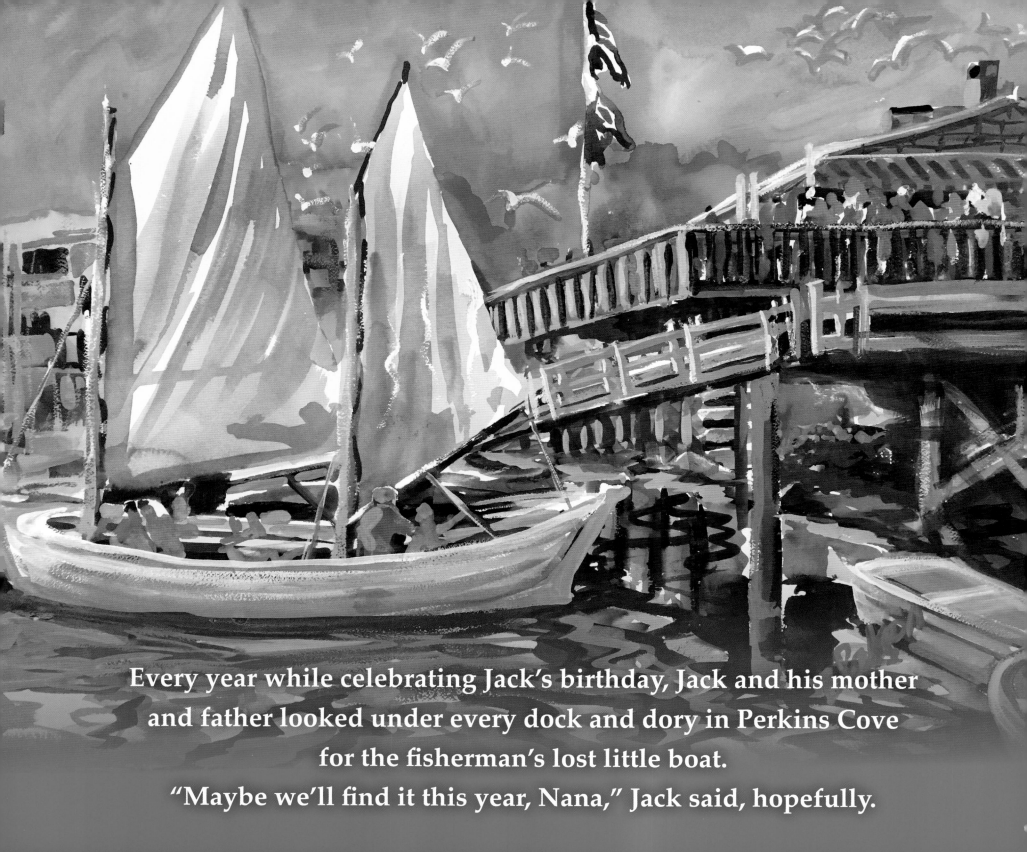

Every year while celebrating Jack's birthday, Jack and his mother
and father looked under every dock and dory in Perkins Cove
for the fisherman's lost little boat.
"Maybe we'll find it this year, Nana," Jack said, hopefully.

They left Nana's house and walked over the footbridge to the cove.
Jack pushed the button to open the bridge and let
a boat with a tall tower pass through.

The first stop they made in the cove was
"Barnacle Billy's."
They sat outside on a deck overlooking the harbor.

As Jack ate lobster, Barnacle Billy
walked over to their table and
told Jack about a huge bluefin
tuna that he helped catch. And Jack told
Billy about the fisherman's boat he hoped to find.

After lunch Jack and his parents waved good-bye to Billy and walked along a path called The Marginal Way. While they walked, Jack looked behind blueberry bushes for the fisherman's boat.

He peeked under the wildflowers and searched beneath a bench, but he did not find it.

They cooled their feet in the clear water of a tide pool.
Jack picked up snails and starfish. He wanted to keep a crab, but
he decided it should stay in nature just like he had learned in school.

At Little Beach near The Marginal Way Jack and his parents swam and jumped in the waves.

They climbed on rocks and searched for seaglass, but they did not find the boat. In the distance Jack spotted something red in the seaweed. He ran to it but found only a lobster claw. "Maybe we'll find it next year," Jack said sadly.

They walked to the bait wharf where a lobsterman
was unloading crates of lobsters.
Jack's father asked him if he had a good catch that day.

"Today was a very good day," he replied. "I even caught a blue lobster which I'll return to the ocean. It's a female and will produce many baby lobsters." Jack had never seen anything like THAT before!

After eating ice-cream cones from The Lobster Shack, Jack and his parents went for a ride on a boat called *Finestkind*. The captain winked and said to Jack, "Be sure to look for the mermaid under the bridge." Jack did and thought he saw her.

The boat sped up as it left the cove, and spray from the waves got Jack's face wet. They watched a lobsterman pull one of his traps from the ocean. He was in a pretty blue boat named *"Clover."*

"Hi Billy Mac," the captain said.
"Can we see your catch?"
"A five-pounder in this one," he replied.

A fishing boat passed by on its' way out to sea.

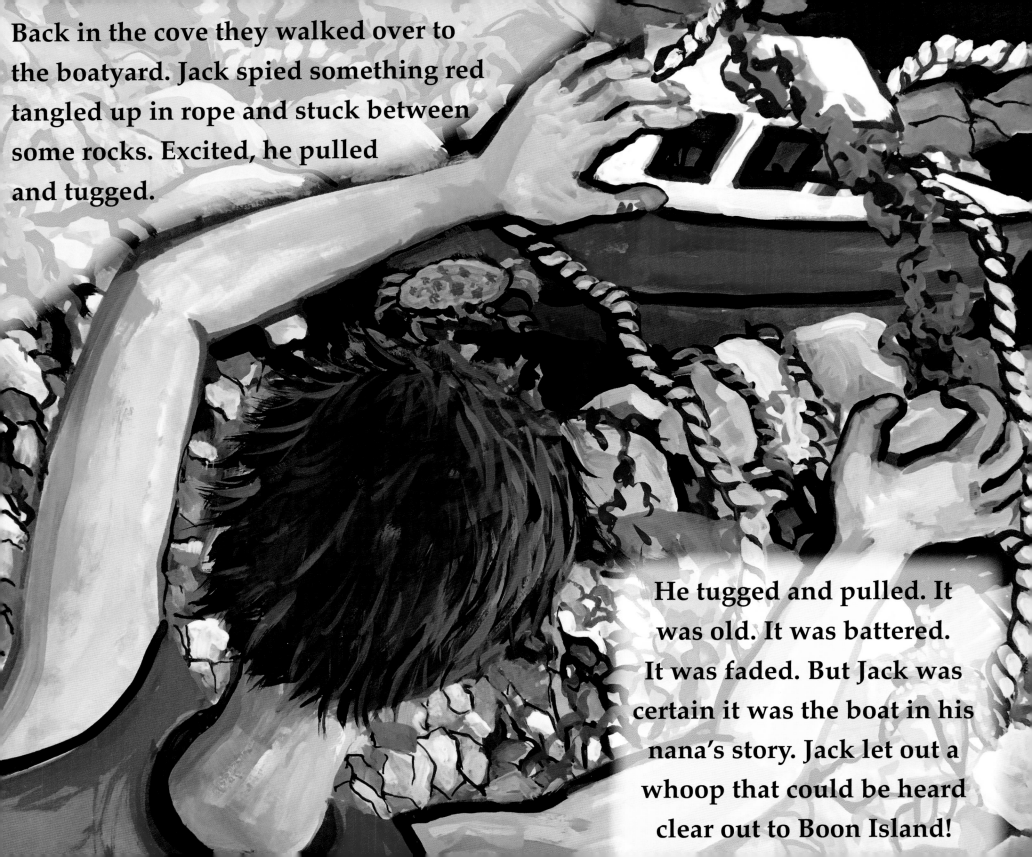

Back in the cove they walked over to the boatyard. Jack spied something red tangled up in rope and stuck between some rocks. Excited, he pulled and tugged.

He tugged and pulled. It was old. It was battered. It was faded. But Jack was certain it was the boat in his nana's story. Jack let out a whoop that could be heard clear out to Boon Island!

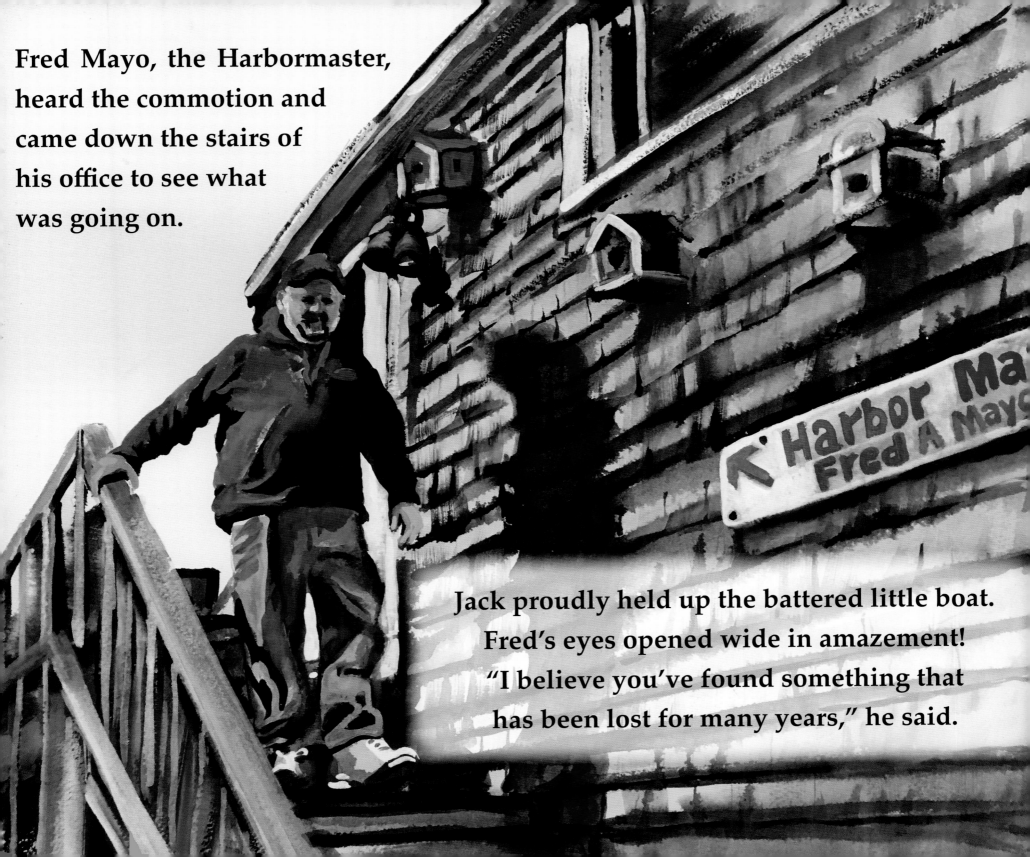

Fred Mayo, the Harbormaster, heard the commotion and came down the stairs of his office to see what was going on.

Jack proudly held up the battered little boat. Fred's eyes opened wide in amazement! "I believe you've found something that has been lost for many years," he said.

"Follow me," said Fred. He pointed to a big red boat surrounded by wildflowers and weeds and resting in a cradle in the corner of the boatyard. "This boat is *'The Crusher'* and hasn't been used for a very long time. *'The Crusher'* was the idea of an old fisherman who carved the boat you found," explained Fred. "The only key we had was lost, and now the townsfolk worry every winter that the bridge will be taken out by the ice like it was so many years ago."

Jack fiddled with the boat. He shook it this way and that, and he heard a rattling sound. He turned the boat over. He pried and pulled. And there inside the boat, just like his nana said, was the secret compartment. And inside the secret compartment was a key.

Fred smiled as Jack held up the key.

They boarded *"The Crusher"* together.

"Go ahead Jack, put the key in and give it a try," Fred said.

The boat spat.

It sputtered.

It clinked

and chugged.

And finally, after a few tries, it started!

There would be no ice build-up in Perkins

Cove this year, and the bridge would be safe!

When Jack and his parents got back to Nana's house,
Jack held up the boat and smiled.
Nana cried and hugged him. "You found the boat! My
grandfather's boat!" This was Jack's best birthday ever!

When Jack returned to Perkins Cove at Christmas time to visit, Fred told him how proud he was of *"The Crusher"* and gave him a brand-new key.

Jack carefully tucked it back inside the secret compartment that the fisherman, his great, great grandfather had carved with his very own hands so many years before.

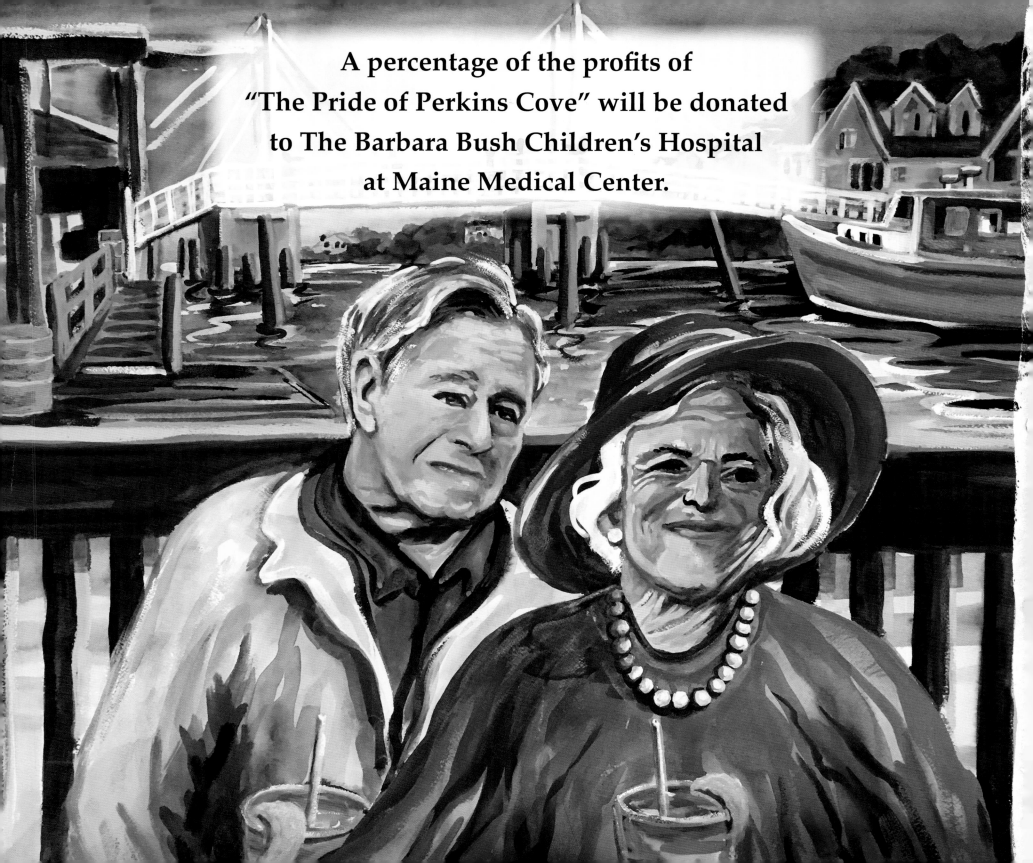

A percentage of the profits of
"The Pride of Perkins Cove" will be donated
to The Barbara Bush Children's Hospital
at Maine Medical Center.